CW01346171

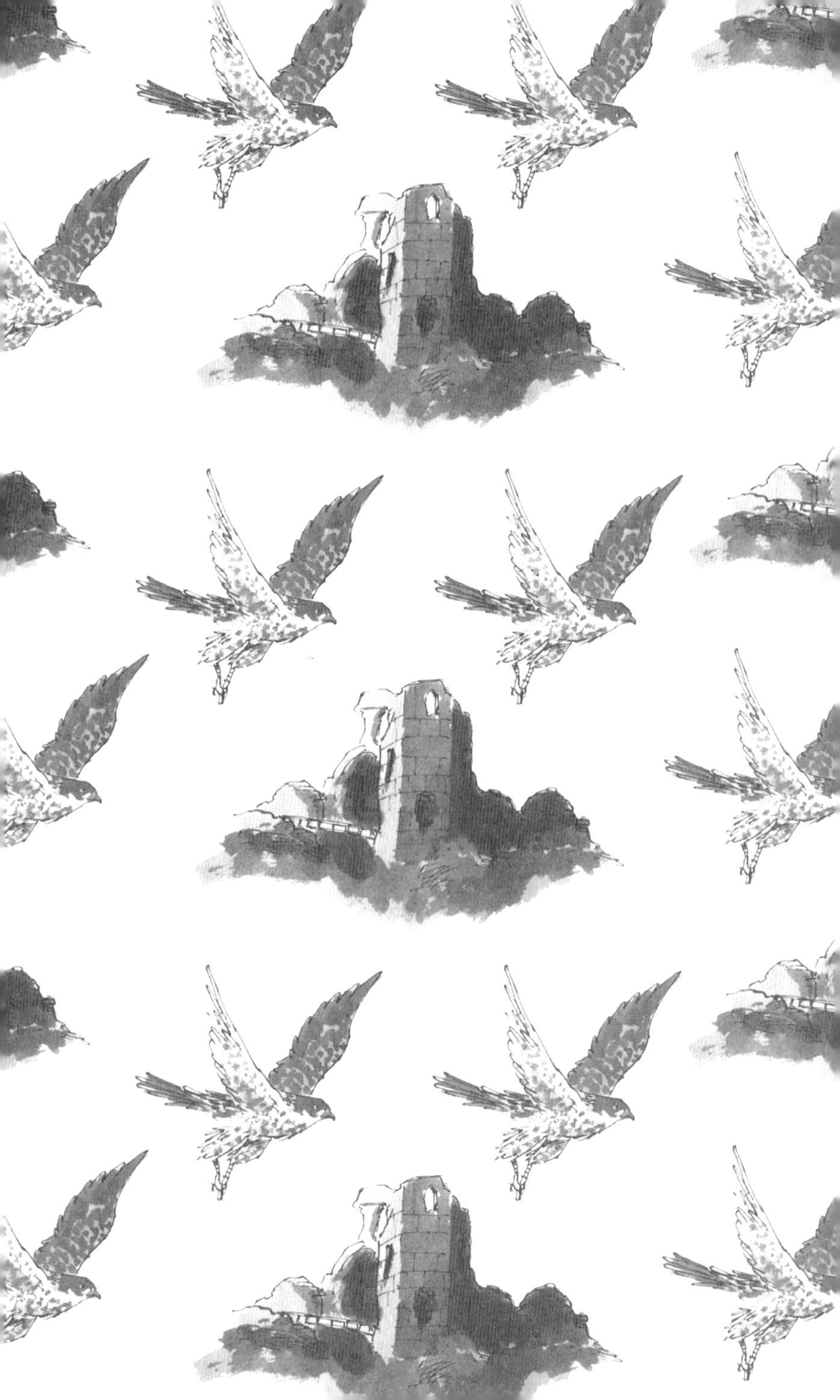

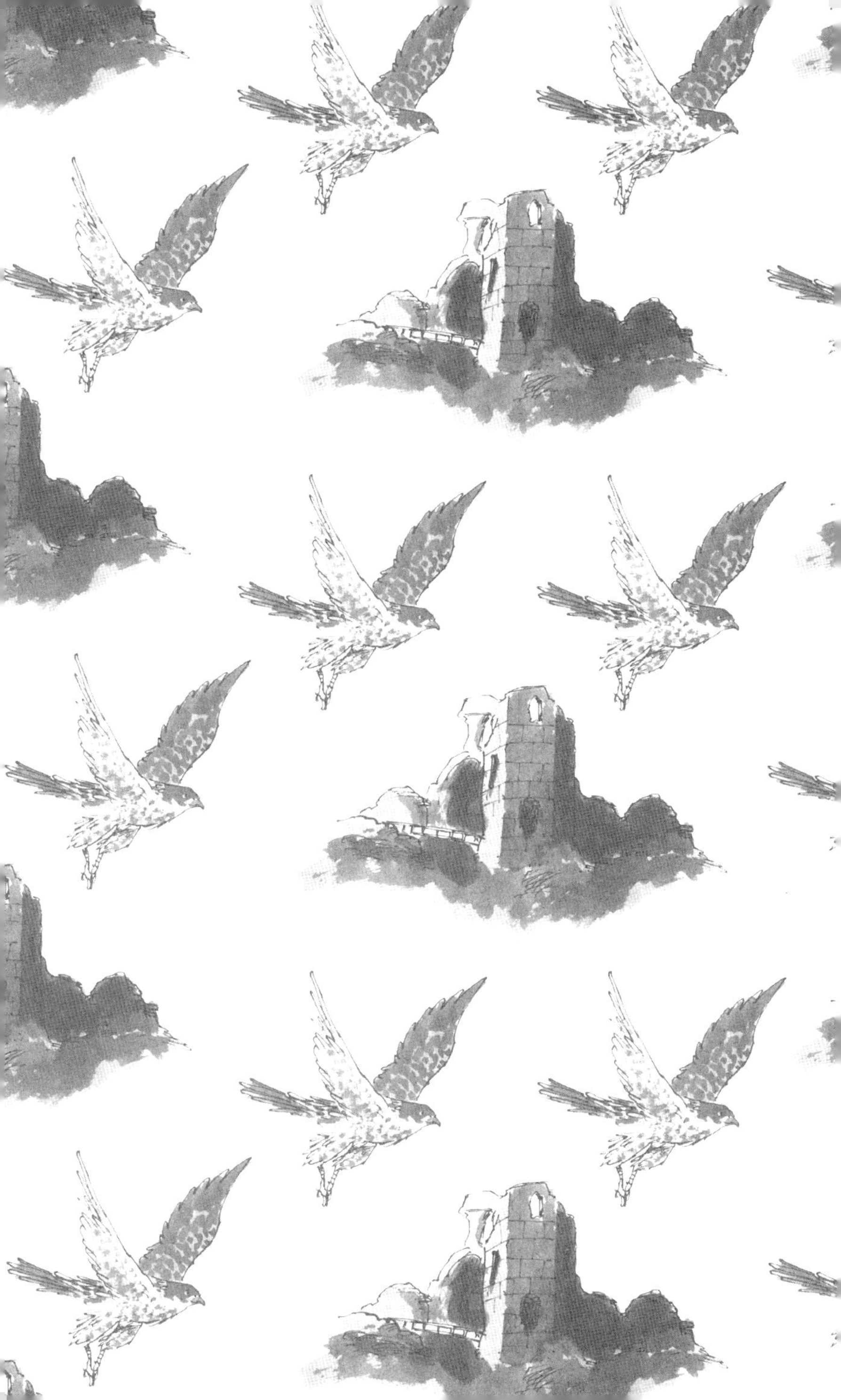

# Saving Anwen

# Saving Anwen

**Oliver Sykes**

Illustrated by
**Ian Morris**

# Collins

# Chapter 1

"New job, fresh start," Andrew says to Mum for what feels like the thousandth time. "I'm turning things round, you'll see."

"Uh-huh," Mum replies, without lifting her head from where she's resting it on the car window.

"I am, Delyth," he insists. "Honest. Things are on the up."

"You just missed the turn," I chip in from the back seat; it's the first thing I've said all journey because Mum's boyfriend Andrew – in typical Andrew-style – has done nothing but talk about himself for the past 20 minutes. He doesn't answer. Of course he doesn't. If there's one thing he hates more than making a mistake, it's being called out for making one.

I cup my hands around my mouth and say, "Hello? Earth to Andrew Connors!"

"Quiet, Griff," scolds Mum. She turns around in her seat and gives me a stare. When she turns back, she places her hand on Andrew's and in her softest voice she says to him, "He's right, love. The turn was back – "

"I KNOW, Delyth!" Andrew replies in his usual stressed tones.

*What does Mum see in him?* I ask myself. *And why does she let him talk to her like that?*

He drives on for another minute, muttering under his breath, while Mum and I sit in awkward silence. When he stops to turn the car around, it lurches forwards. Momentarily, his hard, blue eyes meet mine in the rear-view mirror, sparking that usual feeling of sullen dread in my heart.

The funny thing is, today is supposed to be a day *for me*. The whole point of us taking this trip to Denbigh Castle is so that *I* can get what Mrs Everett, my school counsellor, calls "closure".

You see, my grandad passed away two weeks ago.

It's strange to think that he's not here anymore. Every time I come home, I expect to find him in the living room perched on the edge of his rocking chair or milling about inside the shed at the bottom of our garden. I expect him to see me and for his face to light up, and then for him to ask me about my day, and I can't wait to tell him all about it as fast as I can because then I get to ask him all about his day too … But those days are gone now.

Grandad left behind a letter for me. In it, he asked me to do one thing for him when he was gone. And that was to look after Anwen.

Anwen is a peregrine falcon. She was also his best mate, who he rescued and rewilded some years back. Every night after he saved her, Anwen visited the shed at the bottom of our garden. Grandad used to sit with her for hours and hours by candlelight with his little paraffin stove and a cup of hot chocolate. Whenever he thought she was looking thin, he'd give her a scrap of meat.

You see, peregrine falcons are quite vulnerable, especially when they're young. They need to eat about two small birds a day, so if they're injured and they're struggling to hunt, they can just keel over and die. Grandad wasn't going to let that happen. Not for one second. So, the odd scrap of meat turned into regular meals. Anwen's visits soon became longer and more frequent, and as their friendship grew, Grandad started to learn all about falconry. Then, he started training her.

Mum used to say they were like two peas in a pod – until Grandad invited me to join in, making it three.

5

When he died, we were back to two. Suddenly, it was on me to look after Anwen.

But Andrew – in typical Andrew-style – said it was too dangerous for a 12-year-old to look after a falcon alone. And to my shock, Mum agreed.

I tried to explain to them that falcons aren't pets. That Anwen just liked to visit the shed to be with Grandad. That it wasn't dangerous because I'd already spent hours in the shed with her. I tried to explain to them that the shed was Anwen's home as much as ours. And if they were that concerned, they ought to help me out rather than stop me from fulfilling Grandad's last wish. But they wouldn't listen.

When I came home from school one day, Andrew told me that he'd given Anwen to his mate, Rhys, who runs a company called "Fantastic Falcons".

*I didn't even get to say goodbye!*

And it didn't take more than five minutes for Andrew to take over the shed for his own use either – for yet another one of his destined-to-fail business ventures.

I was upset. Mum was livid.

I felt like I'd let Grandad down.

I still do.

That's about the time Mrs Everett and I started having our one-to-one chats.

In fact, it was Mrs Everett who suggested this trip to Denbigh Castle for the Medieval Festival. As well as live combat training and lots of themed activities, the folk at Fantastic Falcons pitch their own tent, where people can pay to have their photo taken with a bird of prey. It sounds awful to me but if they're as good with animals as Andrew claims, and if Anwen's happy there, then I guess that's the best I can hope for. At least I'll be able to say goodbye to Anwen knowing she's got a good life ahead of her, and who knows? Maybe that will give me the "closure" I'm looking for?

"I can't wait for this," Mum's now saying. "You like knowing the history of things, so I'm sure you're excited to see the castle. Maybe you'll meet some new kids and see Anwen with all her new feathery friends."

Andrew snorts.

Mum ignores him. "How are you feeling, love?" she asks me.

I tell her I'm excited and I try to put on a brave face, but the truth is, I'm feeling really sick. Friends (or rather my lack of any) is starting to become a regular topic of conversation, especially since Grandad passed away, but all I can think about right now is Anwen.

I stare out of the window. The sky darkens. Raindrops start racing down.

"Another cold and drizzly day," grumbles Andrew.

"That's OK," says Mum, trying her best to inject a sliver of positivity into the trip. "We've got coats and umbrellas."

Andrew groans. The car engine joins in too as we trundle uphill. A minute later, we emerge from a narrow street and enter a clearing.

The remains of a huge medieval tower loom over us. The brick has a strange greenish tint to it, which is interesting. I reach for my book, *Castles of North Wales*, and flick through the pages until I come to a double-spread that shows a map of Denbigh Castle and the grounds surrounding it. I find where we are.

"'St Hilary's Chapel,'" I read aloud. "'Sitting a stone's throw away from the castle grounds,'" I continue, "'only the tower now survives of the chapel that served the market town for six centuries. The tower is made of greenish Gwespyr stone, which was also used in the construction of the Green Chambers within the castle grounds, probably around the mid-14th century.' Cool."

Suddenly, Andrew slams on the brakes. The force pushes my body into my seatbelt, sending my book flying.

"Blimey, Andrew!" groans Mum. "There was no need for that."

"Sorry," he replies, getting out of the car. "My foot slipped."

# Chapter 2

As I climb out of the car, fierce rain strikes my face. I turn my back to it, slip my book inside my coat pocket, and pull up my hood.

Sixty metres ahead of us, there's a huge flagpole that sticks out of one of the castle towers; I can see the flag of Wales. It might be sopping wet, but it still dances proudly in the wind, the green and the red sticking out against the dull grey sky.

"Hurry up," orders Andrew, trudging away ahead of us. That's when I first take in what he's wearing: the same baggy hoodie and tracksuit bottoms that he's been wearing all week. I can't remember the last time Andrew took that big grey beanie off. "Hurry up," he shouts, louder this time.

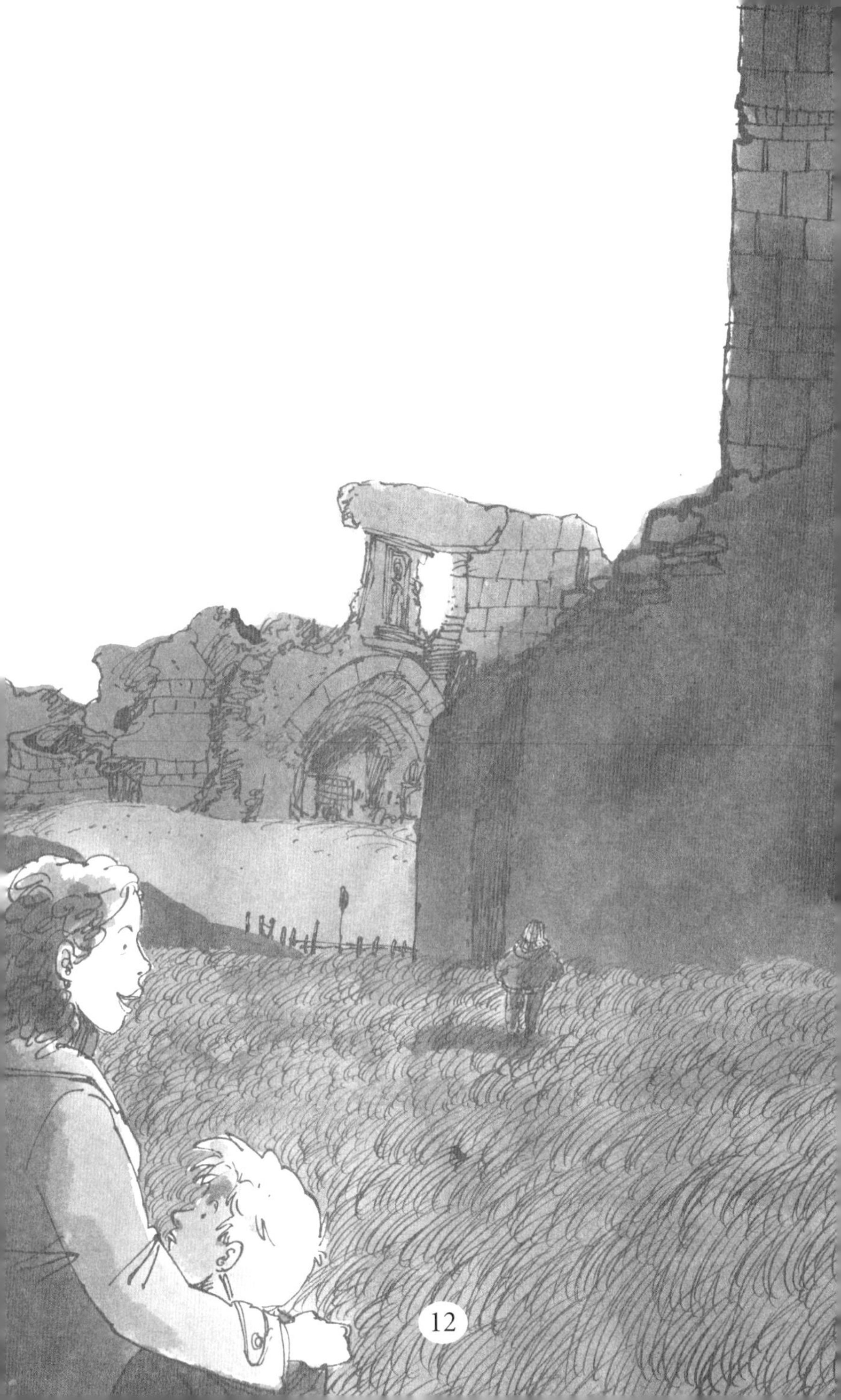

Mum crouches down to use the car's side mirror to check her lipstick. She's wearing her smart bright-purple coat and her hiking boots. "How do I look?" she asks.

"Lovely," I reply.

Seeing Andrew all grubby, stalking off without a care in the world, while she's so determined to look her best, makes me feel sad. In a way, it kind of sums up their relationship. I don't think I've ever heard Andrew say that Mum looks nice or compliment her on being kind or smart, which she is, all the time.

Mum opens her umbrella, pulls me under it and links her arm through mine. "We're coming," she calls to Andrew, as we make our way uphill.

Soon, we're treading over an old, wooden drawbridge, gazing up at the spectacular entrance – the great triple-towered gatehouse. It's so impressive, far better than the photos in my book. It makes me wonder how humans were ever able to build something so big and so grand. It must have taken AGES!

A sudden thundering sound snaps me out of

my thoughts; the rattling chains of the portcullis being raised. Only nothing's moving at all …

The sound gets louder and louder – closer and closer.

I tear my arm away from Mum, jump to the side and duck by the guardrail. When I dare to look up, I hear the sound of horses and marching soldiers. It's only then that I realise *it's not real*! I've activated a sensor on the wall that plays these sounds to everyone who enters!

"Heart of a lion, that one," Andrew jokes, offering Mum his hand.

"Leave him be," she replies.

She takes his hand and they walk side-by-side.

I've got to say, judging by their clothing alone, they make a very ODD pair …

I follow them inside the gatehouse. To the left is a big red-and-white sign bolted into the wall, which says "DANGER: Do not climb on the walls".

*Climb on the walls?* I think to myself. *I am not going to be doing that, even if I was being chased!*

We make our way to the edge of the castle grounds, where I see a big grassy lawn about the size of a football pitch.

Dotted all around the edge of the lawn are people in big, waterproof coats, standing at stalls: some are selling food and drink, some are doing face-painting and crafts, some are selling sweets and toys. And the lawn is heaving with children too. It's crowded and noisy, like a fair. There must be 200 people here, at least.

One half of the lawn is filled with seats and tables. That bit is mostly empty. But the other half looks like a cross between a busy school playground and a medieval battlefield: kids, some dressed normally, some dressed as knights, are chasing one another, crashing wooden swords and axes together. I guess this has something to do with medieval combat training but it's a scene of utter chaos.

Out of nowhere, a loud wailing sound cuts through the din – "ghiii – ghiii – ghiii!".

Everyone cranes their heads to the overcast sky, including me.

Amid the dark grey clouds and the drizzle of rain, we watch as a small, tethered bird circles and scans the grounds below. The bird angles its wings, slips sideways for three or so metres, flutters, and then starts to hover again.

"Is that her?" asks Mum. "Is that Anwen?"

"I hope not," I reply. "That bird's attached to a creance."

Mum shrugs her shoulders at me. "A what, now?"

"A long cord," I say. "You tether it to the bird, so it doesn't fly off. Grandad said you're only supposed to use them to fly a bird between a perch and your fist. I don't think you're supposed to use them to fly a bird *like that*. And not in this weather too."

"Ah, I see," says Mum, staring up at the sky.

"Here's a thought," interrupts Andrew. "Maybe the falconry experts know a little bit more than a 12-year-old boy and his grandad, eh? Wouldn't that be something?"

"Andrew," says Mum, disapprovingly. "Please, be nice."

"All right," he grumbles, clearly not meaning it.

"There's only one way to find out," I reply, staring up at him. "I say we go find these falconry '*experts*', and talk to them."

Andrew just shrugs and carries on walking.

Before I know it, we're through the warm, dry, gift shop and back outside in the cold, wet, castle grounds.

Suddenly, the rain stops. As I look up at the sky, I notice that whoever was flying that bird has called it back in.

*Good,* I think to myself.

I lower my hood and run my hand through my hair.

Mum closes her umbrella. "Fingers crossed for a spot of sun."

Andrew moans, "Fat chance of that – "

"Right," says Mum, cutting him off. "Who wants a hot drink?"

"Aye. Go on, then," says Andrew.

"Mum, can I go and find Anwen?" I ask, tugging her coat sleeve. All this waiting is making me feel anxious.

"Wait," snaps Andrew. He fishes into his pocket, pulls out a thick wad of banknotes, peels one off and hands it to my mum. "How about you get us some drinks while I go and chat to Rhys? I'm going to see if we can get Griff some time with Anwen, so they can have a proper goodbye."

*What?* My heart starts thumping inside my chest. *Why is Andrew suddenly pretending to care about me? And Anwen? Something's wrong.*

"Sure," says Mum, oblivious to this new development. "That would be lovely."

She wanders off in the direction of the stalls, leaving Andrew and me alone.

When she's ten or so steps away, Andrew lets out a long, low sigh. "Right," he says. "Let's get this over and done with."

We walk-race through the middle of the lawn, swerving swinging sword-bearers and evading clumsy axe-wielders. When we're halfway there, I spot the bright red Fantastic Falcons gazebo. Next to it, is a big brown tent. Neither are in good shape. The gazebo is old and worn and sagging in the middle. And some of the lettering has peeled right off, so it now reads: *Fanta tic Fa con.*

As for the big brown tent, there's a great slit at the front of it that's been crudely repaired with what looks like packing tape.

*That doesn't look great,* I think to myself, but lots of people don't have much money. Maybe Rhys can't afford a new one.

Under the gazebo, there's a tall man wearing a tweed jacket and trousers.

He has close-cropped hair and bushy eyebrows.

My first thought is, *His falconry set-up looks a bit miserable*. But there's no way I'd ever say that to his face. He looks friendly, but something doesn't feel right.

As we join the queue, I ask Andrew if that's Rhys.

"Yup," he says, sounding a bit breathless.

"Are you all right?" I ask, but he ignores me.

Rhys directs a mother and daughter at the front of the queue with a big, booming voice. "Step right up, little girl! Over here!"

The young girl clings to her mum, eyes bulging wide with terror, but her mum ushers her towards him.

"Photo time," he declares, "with one of our fantastic falcons! Quickly, Mum, we've not got all day!" He holds out his hand, rubbing his forefingers against his thumb. She hands him some money, which he slips into his pocket. Then, he directs them both to a boy who looks like a miniature version of him, complete with close-cropped hair, tweed jacket and trousers.

"This here is Troy," says Rhys, proudly, clapping Troy on the back. "He may be young, but he's very skilled and wise. Just like his dad."

Rhys lets out a big belly-laugh, and Troy takes the mother and daughter to the front of the big brown tent. That's when I first catch sight of their "fantastic" falcons.

My heart drops.

The hobby and the kestrel seem OK, but the peregrine falcon looks pitiful. Before Andrew gave Anwen away, she was big from being so well-fed; every feather looked like it had been polished, whereas this bird looks rough, underfed and utterly dejected. They're each tethered to a rusty-looking bow perch; I can see the falcon flapping its wings listlessly.

*There's no way I can let Anwen live like this*, I tell myself, feeling the nerves beginning to rise in my chest. *Someone ought to call the RSPB.*

After a moment thinking, the girl points at the miserable falcon standing on the furthest perch. Troy places a mud-splattered raptor glove over the girl's right hand and repositions her using the brown tent as a backdrop for her photograph.

Just as he goes to pick up the falcon, it cocks its head towards me and holds my gaze with its piercing yellow eyes.

I lean in a bit closer. *Wait a minute … I've seen those eyes before!* I do a double-take. "Anwen?" I whisper. *I don't believe it! That's her!*

# Chapter 3

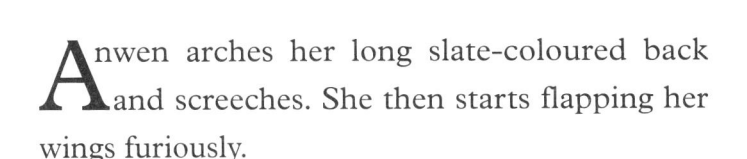

Anwen arches her long slate-coloured back and screeches. She then starts flapping her wings furiously.

Rather than attempting to work out what's happening or trying to distract her, putting a hood on her or simply leaving her be, Troy tries to wrestle the glove's leather ties to the anklet on her leg.

Anwen squawks. Not in fear but in indignation.

I give it a moment, trusting Andrew's word that these people are good with birds, hoping Troy will back off, but he doesn't. He ignores all of Anwen's signs of distress.

*What is he doing? He's going to get –*

Then, it happens.

One quick flash of Anwen's needle-sharp talons and Troy receives a scratch across his right cheek. He lets out a squawk of his own.

Seeing this, the girl pulls her hand free of the raptor glove and runs back to her mother.

Meanwhile, Anwen paces back and forth on her ring-perch, clearly agitated.

With a face flushed red with anger, the mother marches over to Rhys and demands her money back. I can't hear what Rhys is saying exactly but I don't have to. The hard expression on his face clearly says, "No refunds". The mother raises her voice and points her finger at him until Rhys stands to his full height, towering over her. This brings the conversation to a close. And it feels … wrong. Part of me wants to speak up and help her out, but he sounds really frightening and I don't dare.

As the mother stomps past us back into the crowd, pulling her daughter along with her, I hear her mutter something about calling the RSPB.

*Good,* I think. *I hope she does.*

Suddenly, the atmosphere around the Fantastic Falcons tent feels really uncomfortable. The people standing in front of us exchange nervous looks and then walk away too, leaving Andrew and me at the front of the queue.

Rhys is barking orders at Troy. "Get inside with that bird, now!" he shouts.

"What? And have her scratch the other side of my face?" Troy replies, pointing at his cheek. "I can't, Dad. I'm too scared. You'll have to do it."

Rhys charges over to Anwen.

*No! Don't hurt her!* I think. I move towards them, but Andrew holds me back, clutching the front of my coat. I try to shrug him off, but he only tightens his grip.

After several clumsy attempts to place a small hood over Anwen's head, Rhys finally manages it. The effect is instant. Anwen stands still and relaxed, as if the last couple of minutes had never happened.

I'm waiting for Rhys to give Anwen a reward for accepting the hood but instead he turns his back on her.

"Give her a reward!" I shout, without meaning to.

Rhys whips around and stares daggers at me.

I look away.

"Uh-oh," mutters Andrew.

"What do you mean, 'Uh-oh'?" I ask, under my breath. "I thought you said he was your friend?"

Andrew says nothing.

The big man starts pacing towards me, menacingly. He's quite close, when Andrew takes a deep breath and pulls his beanie up a bit.

"Hey, Rhys! How are you, mate?"

Rhys stops in his tracks and does a double-take. "You!" he exclaims. His face then falls back into a scowl. "How am I?" he asks, in a mocking tone. "Absolutely chipper, Andrew. Tip top. Couldn't be happier."

"Oh, yeah?" Andrew replies.

"NO!" roars Rhys, making Andrew visibly quake with fear. "Maybe I'm mistaken, *mate*, but I remember you saying that bird of yours was tame?

Look at these!" He holds up his hands for us to see. Across his left palm, there's a deep gash, and there are several deep scratches across the fingers of his right hand too.

I'm wondering why he's been handling a new falcon without taking the proper precautions, when he adds: "Worst buy of my life!"

For a moment, nobody says anything.

"*Buy?*" I say, looking up at Andrew.

"It's a saying," he replies.

"Anyway," declares Rhys, leaning down to me. His lips are so close to my face I can feel his breath. "I suppose this is Griff?"

"Er – yeah," murmurs Andrew, pushing me forward.

"You want to see my new bird, do you?" Rhys asks.

I try to hold his fierce gaze but I can't.

"You did say that was OK, didn't you?" asks Andrew, timidly.

*What's going on?* I ask myself, unable to describe how strange this feels. *If, ten minutes ago, you'd have asked me to describe Andrew in one word, there's a good chance I'd have said, "Bully", and yet, here he is being bullied himself by someone much bigger, tougher and meaner than him.*

"Let's see those hands of yours then, Griff," says Rhys. Before I can say "no", he grips them firmly in his and starts turning them over, inspecting them. "Hah! Not a scratch on them," he blasts, looking up at Andrew. Then, he looks me in the eye. "You've not handled that bird!"

"I have," I reply, stepping away. "Quite a lot, too. Anwen's not difficult if – "

"What sort of a name is Arwen?" he asks, cutting me off.

"It's not Arwen. It's Anwen," I tell him. "My grandad gave her that name after he saved her life – "

"Well, Griff," he says, really drawing out my name. "How about I let you in on a little secret? That grandad of yours might have done us all a favour if he'd just left little Anwen to fend for herself, 'cos that right there is the worst bird I've ever seen, let alone worked with."

Just then, Troy trudges over and scans Andrew from head to toe. "That's the man who sold her to us, isn't it, Dad?"

"Quiet, you," scolds Rhys.

"Sold?" I say, turning to Andrew. "So, they *did* buy Anwen. What's really going on here?"

Andrew takes a deep breath. "All right," he replies. "Rhys here just gave me a little something for my trouble."

But I can see Andrew winking at Rhys, almost begging him to agree. "Some cash," Andrew continues, "to cover my expenses to deliver Anwen, you know, petrol and stuff. That's all."

"Petrol?" scoffs Troy. "Yeah, maybe if you drove here from Russia!"

"Ha! That's true," Rhys says. "Now, get that bird inside, so this little boy can – very quickly – say his goodbyes to that rat with wings. Right? Move!"

I glare up at Andrew, who looks away.

"Listen," says Andrew to Rhys, whilst steering me away, "while Troy's sorting that, I'm just going to have a quick chat with Griff, yeah?"

Rhys grumbles something about hurrying up.

"Now, listen here, Griff," says Andrew, gripping my right shoulder.

*There's literally nothing he can say to convince me to leave Anwen with that monster … Nothing!*

"Since your grandad died, and since I lost my job, things have been hard for your mum. Yeah? She needs money to pay for all sorts of stuff – food, rent, bills, car, you – and all I want to do is help her out, yeah, help us out."

Unsure where he's going with this, I simply nod.

"But this bird," he continues, "she's not helping. You know that, don't you?"

I start to protest but he cuts me off.

"We can't keep her, Griff, and that's final. We haven't got the time. We haven't got the space.

We haven't got the cash. And when you add all that together, in that head of yours, then, you'll understand."

"Understand, what?"

"Why I had to sell her," he says, and he's staring at the ground, unable to even look me in the eye.

I clench my fists. "WHAT?"

Behind Andrew, I notice Rhys is staring right at us. But I don't care. I'm so angry I shout, "I'm telling my mum, and we're taking Anwen back, and if anyone tries to stop us, I'll call the RSPB."

"Shush," says Andrew, tightening his grip on my shoulder until it starts to hurt. "Look, they've got plenty of birds here, Griff. Rhys has been in business for as long as you've been alive, and he knows what he's doing. That bird – she'll go her way. We'll go ours."

"That bird," I shout, "has a name. And that name is Anwen. You heard what he called her – a rat with wings!"

"Yeah, he did," acknowledges Andrew, "but that's Rhys's sense of humour. He's only having a laugh. The point is, we'll put the money he gave me to good use. It'll tide us over until I find a new job, yeah?"

"New job?" I say. "But, in the car, you said – "

"We'll be working together to help your mum out, Griff. Doesn't that sound good? Doesn't that sound like something your grandad would've wanted? And, check this out, right. What if I sweeten the deal by getting you that new pair of trainers you were asking your mum for? Eh? That wouldn't be too bad, would it? What do you say, mate?"

I don't know what to say.

*How can he possibly care about Anwen, when he SOLD her?*

*He's a liar.*

*He doesn't care about anyone but himself.*

*He doesn't even have a new job.*

*And here he is now, trying to cover his tracks, trying to lie his way out of it! Well, not if I have anything to do with it.*

"All right, then," I lie. "You get me those new trainers and you've got yourself a deal."

"Thatta boy!" says Andrew, clapping me on the back.

As soon as he steps away, I try to make a run for it.

"No! Griff!" he shouts, clutching my coat sleeve. "We have a deal! Wait! Wait!"

"Don't let him go!" shouts Rhys.

I swing my arms wildly. Andrew lets go. I tear away, making a break for it.

# Chapter 4

After three or four long strides, I hit a solid wall of play-fighting children.

*Oh no! He's going to catch me!* I think, freezing in panic.

I steal a quick glance over my shoulder and see Andrew rushing towards me with his arm outstretched. I let out a high-pitched shriek, which makes him, and those around us, stop.

I don't know where it comes from, but I find myself pointing at Andrew, shouting, "Warriors! This man wants to lock you all in the dungeons!"

The kids look at me.

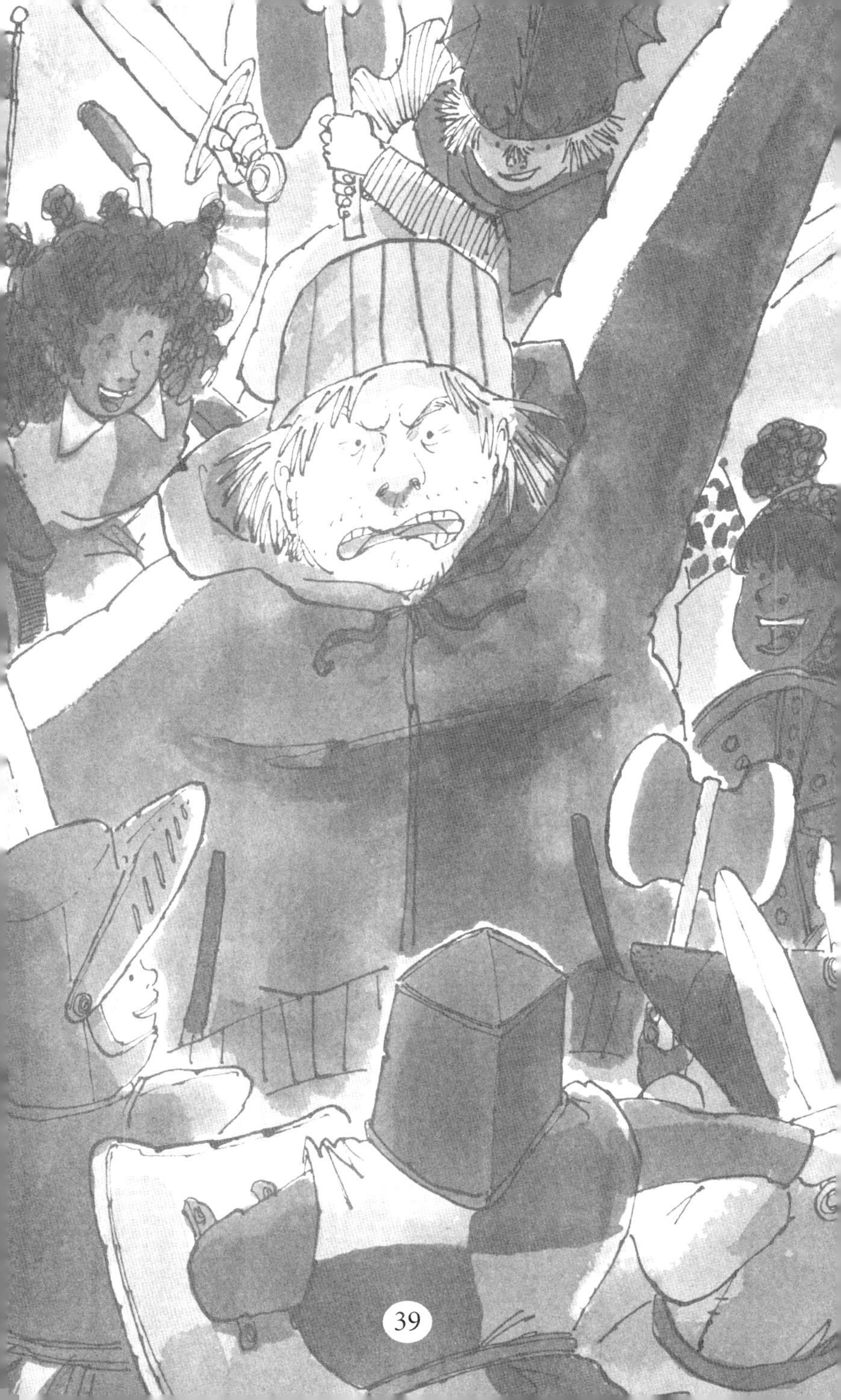

"We don't want that, do we?" I shout again.

"No," they reply.

Andrew takes a quick step back.

"All of you!" I call out. "GET HIM!"

Andrew's eyes bulge wide with horror as a wave of children charge at him, wielding their weapons and screaming warrior cries. The last thing I see is Andrew, surrounded by children, his arms flailing, before he hits the ground with a crunch. Back at the falconry tent, Rhys is staring right at me, angrily shaking his head.

I turn on my heels and sprint to the middle of the lawn as fast as I can.

I look for Mum as I weave in and out of people, passing stand after stand – freshly-made sandwiches, pancakes, vegetable samosas, fresh doughnuts, candy floss – but there's no sign of her anywhere. Suddenly, I spot a flash of bright purple in the crowd.

"Mum!" I shout.

I look back over my shoulder and spot

Andrew, angrily marching towards us with Rhys following.

I've never been so scared in all my life. I position myself behind Mum.

"Griff, what is it?" asks Mum, impatiently.

"It's them!" I point.

"What?" she asks, turning her head. "What on earth has happened?"

"Andrew's a liar, Mum," I say, tugging on her arm. "He's sold her to that man!"

"Slow down," says Mum. "Sold who? Wait, is this about Anwen?"

"Of course it's about Anwen!" I say, but it's more like a shout, and my shout makes Mum flinch, but I can't help it. "This whole day is supposed to be about Anwen, and it's not! It's about him! It's always about him! And he doesn't care! He doesn't care about you or me or anybody but himself!"

Just then, Andrew and Rhys arrive.

My stomach tightens, but I don't let that stop me. I point right at Andrew, and I shout, "You're a liar!" And then I point at Rhys. "And you're mistreating Anwen!"

"Now, hold on," says Andrew, holding his hands up in the air. "Listen. Griff, you're confused, mate."

"No, I'm not," I cry angrily.

"Rhys?" adds Andrew, looking for support.

"I'm sorry about this little misunderstanding," he says, nodding towards me like I'm the problem.

I stare up at Mum.

"I'm afraid Griff here is a little confused." Rhys bends down to my level. "I'm sorry, Griff, but you are, mate. You got the wrong end of the stick. Nothing to be ashamed of."

*Mum clearly believes every word he's saying.*

"No," I cry, swallowing hard, my heart pounding. "You're lying!"

Rhys rises up to his full height. "Griff thinks Andrew *sold* Anwen to me for lots of money," he says, with a chuckle. "But we're practically a charity. We haven't got lots of money. No. What happened was, he heard some talk of money, and then the poor boy thought it meant something else. The truth is, I gave Andrew here a small amount to cover his petrol, that's all. I mean, that's what mates do, isn't it?"

It's only then that I realise tears are falling down my face. "You're both liars," I stammer.

Mum gives my shoulder a squeeze. "That all makes sense. Listen, I think Griff and I need a quiet moment. Excuse us."

We've only taken a few steps when she stops and turns around. "No, Andrew," she adds. "Just me and Griff."

Mum leads me away to the edge of the lawn.

*She must believe me!* I tell myself.

"They're lying, Mum," I sob. "Not just about Anwen but about everything. Andrew doesn't even have a job!"

Mum closes her eyes and breathes loudly once through her nose. "Please. Not this again, Griff," she says. "Ever since Andrew came into our lives, all you've done is complain. Don't forget he did drive us here. He's trying to turn his life around – for us."

44

"But, Mum?" I stammer. "You weren't there. That man, Rhys, called Anwen a rat with wings."

"Come on, now," she says. "Even if he did say that, I'm sure he was only joking. Look, Mrs Everett made it very clear to us that this trip might be too much too soon. What happens with Anwen is important, Griff, but it's not as important as you."

"No, Mum. No. You've got it all wrong – " I try to say.

"We're going home, Griff. We can always visit Anwen another time when you're feeling better. OK?"

I wipe the tears from my eyes with my coat sleeve and take a step away from her. "No."

Mum glares at me and I glare back. "Excuse me?" she says.

Another step. "I said, no."

"Griff?" she says, anger and confusion rising in her voice.

"If I leave now, there might not be another time … so, no, Mum … I'm not leaving until I know Anwen is safe."

# Chapter 5

I jump down from the edge of the lawn and run away at full speed, my trainers crunching loudly on the gravel path.

Behind me, I can hear Mum shouting, "Come back here now, Griff! Come back!"

She sounds really upset, but I can't go back. Not until she believes me. Not until I've saved Anwen.

When her voice fades away and I'm sure I'm out of sight, I run straight down some stone steps, past another big red-and-white sign bolted into the wall, which says "DANGER: No climbing", and through a wide aisle with walls on either side of me. Whole sections of these walls have tumbled away and gaps have been left to erode and crumble.

*No wonder they don't want you climbing,* I think. *The whole wall would probably give way!*

I reach a different part of the castle grounds: a much smaller lawn surrounded on three sides by tall stone walls.

Ahead of me, vast farmlands seem to stretch out for miles and miles. I could just run. I could climb down, jump a fence or two, run away and never come back. But I know I can't.

I swallow hard. *Anwen needs me,* I tell myself.

I scurry over to a large chunk of rock that juts out of the ruins. I wipe the tears from my face and sit down to make a plan. Remembering my *Castles of North Wales* book, I fish it out of my coat pocket and turn to the section that contains maps. When I find the map of Denbigh Castle, I try to work out where I am, but the walls around me are so tall and thick and wide, they hide everything within the castle grounds.

I think back to my History lessons,

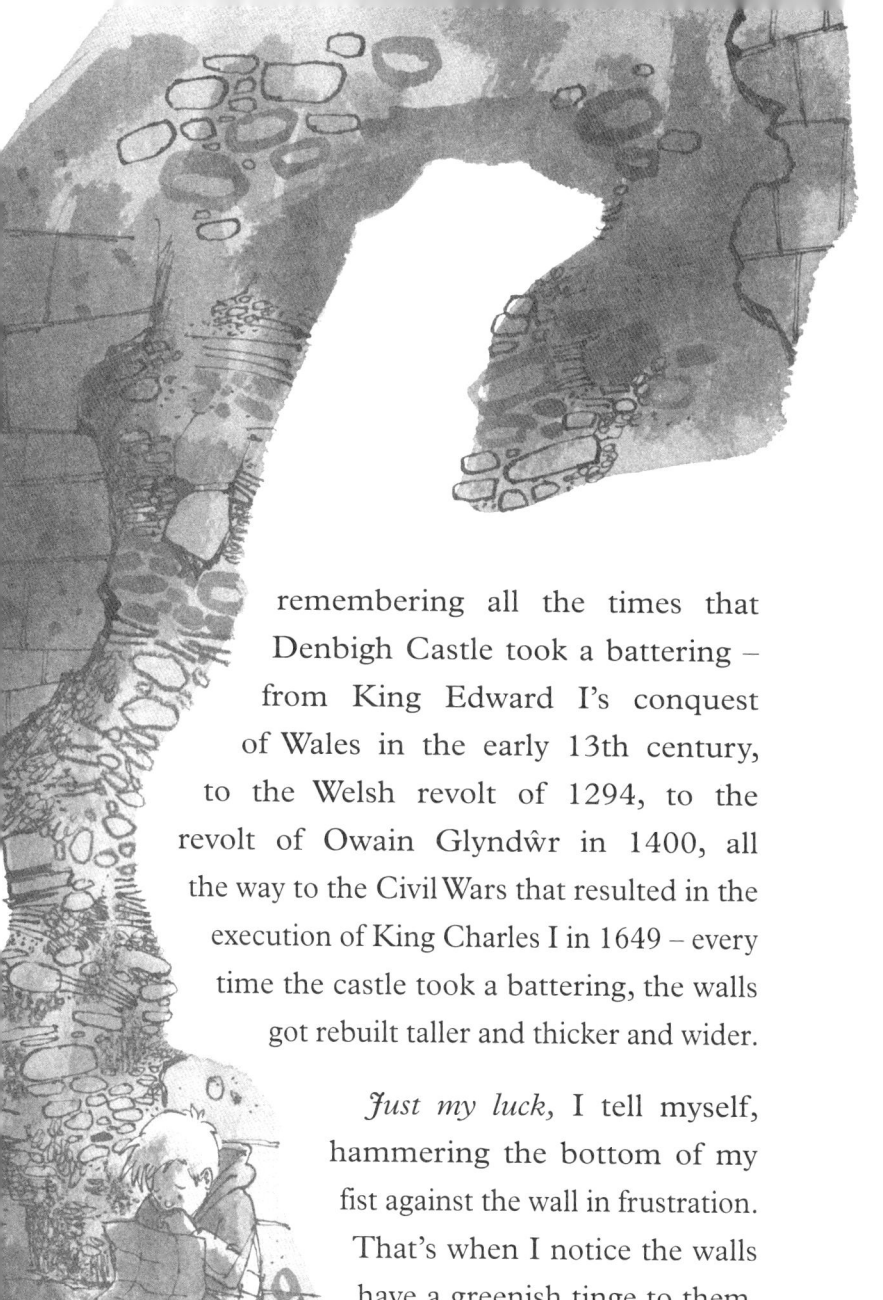

remembering all the times that Denbigh Castle took a battering – from King Edward I's conquest of Wales in the early 13th century, to the Welsh revolt of 1294, to the revolt of Owain Glyndŵr in 1400, all the way to the Civil Wars that resulted in the execution of King Charles I in 1649 – every time the castle took a battering, the walls got rebuilt taller and thicker and wider.

*Just my luck,* I tell myself, hammering the bottom of my fist against the wall in frustration. That's when I notice the walls have a greenish tinge to them, just like the tower we passed in the car.

"The Green Chambers!" I remember. "It's made of Gwespyr stone. Yes! That must be where I am." On the map, there's a small cartoon of a lion's face, which makes me look up and around, and sure enough I see it – a stone carving of a lion's face sticking out of the wall.

Now I know exactly where I am, I use my finger to trace the route to the Fantastic Falcons tent. It's not far, but it's exactly where Mum, Andrew and Rhys will expect me to go next, unless I can disguise myself or cause a diversion.

I pocket my book and head back the way I came to check the coast is clear, but then I hear voices on the other side of the wall.

I instantly recognise Andrew's voice. "I'll find him and put him in the car, and I'll take him home."

"And what about Griff saying he'll contact the RSPB?" That's Rhys, and he sounds really angry. "I paid you good money for that bird," he continues. "If you'd have told me it was going to be this much trouble, I wouldn't have bothered."

"There'll be no more trouble," says Andrew, sounding sullen. "I'll make sure of it. I promise. Whatever it takes."

*Whatever it takes?* I repeat in my head, as I scurry back over to the large chunk of rock and crouch behind it. *What does that mean?*

I feel a strange burning sensation in the pit of my stomach ... Fear. *How am I supposed to stop them? I'm not strong enough.*

"Now, get in there and have a look for him," orders Rhys.

The sound of wet squeaking shoes tells me that Andrew's approaching. I crouch even lower, pressing my back against the wall.

*Please don't find me ... Please don't find me ...*

"Is he there?" asks Rhys.

Each second ticks by like a minute. I can feel my heart thumping against my chest.

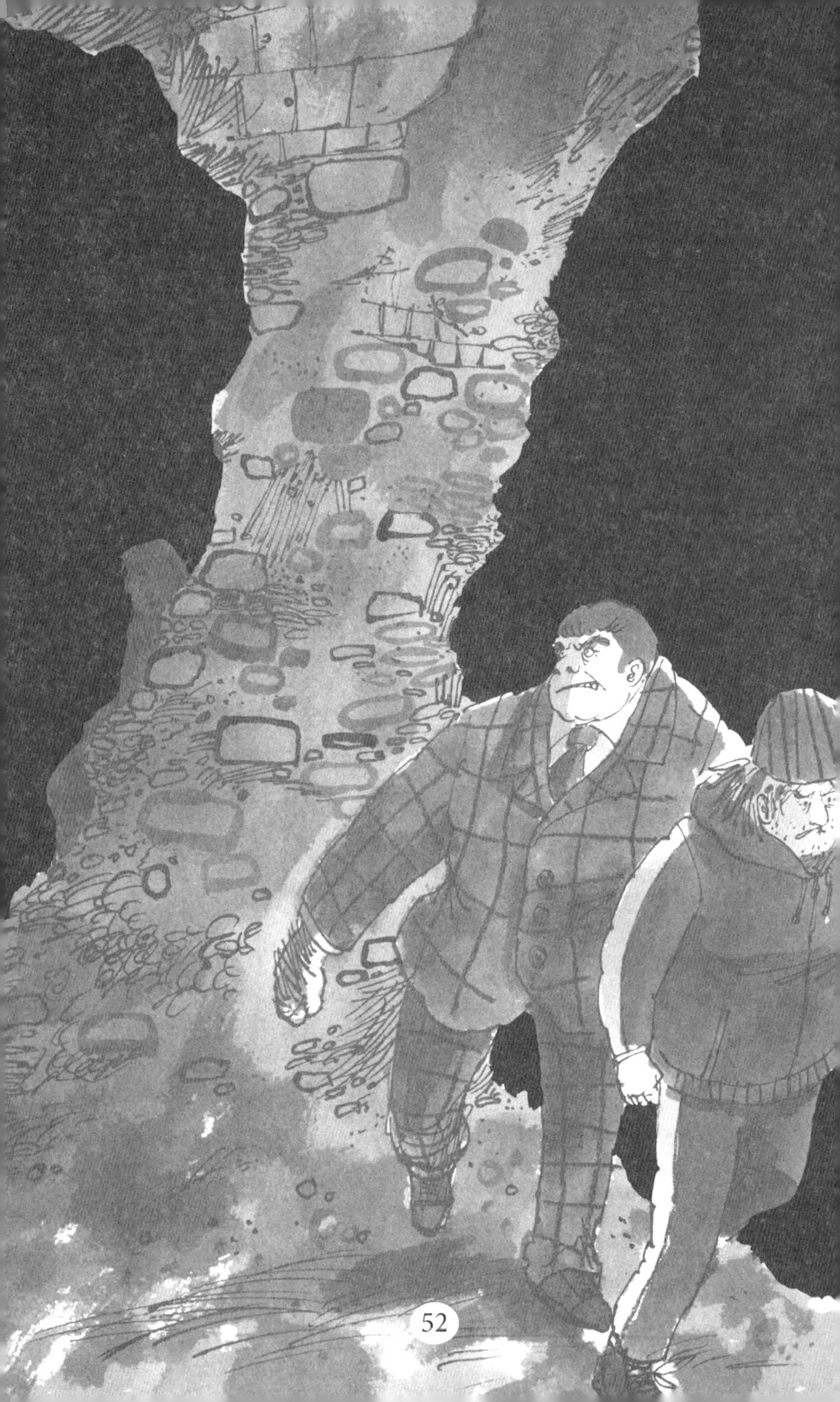

"No," calls Andrew.

"Right," says Rhys. "Back to the tent."

Once they've left, I expect to feel a great wave of relief wash over me, but it doesn't come. Instead, my stomach tightens and I feel a bit sick.

I can't do this alone. I need help. But who's going to help me?

# Chapter 6

I'm trying to think of a solution, when I remember Rhys's son, Troy.

*He didn't exactly want Anwen around,* I tell myself. *Maybe I could use that to my advantage? But what if I ask for his help and he says no? Or worse: what if he gets his dad?*

I begin making my way out of the Green Chambers. All I know is that I need help. I can't do this alone. And, if I'm going to save Anwen, I've got to get a move on.

As I jog past the spot where I heard Andrew and Rhys talking, I take my coat off and turn it inside out before putting it back on. It's been raining so much that it instantly soaks my jumper, but I figure if they're looking for a boy in a green coat, then the bright yellow inner-lining should throw them off.

I turn the corner, place my hand on one of the wall's many jagged cracks, and peer out. The lawn is still teeming with kids. Straight ahead, I can see Andrew and Rhys walking along the path with their backs to me.

I step out and follow close behind a family as cover. When Andrew and Rhys reach the big brown tent, they head straight inside.

Only one bird remains sitting outside on a perch; the other two are empty. As I walk along, I watch carefully as Troy appears from inside the tent. He puts out his hand and the remaining bird – I think it's the hobby but it's hard to tell from this distance – hops onto his glove. He hands her a treat and strokes her breast-feathers with his finger before taking her back inside.

Realising the coast is clear, I break away and dive into some bushes behind the brown tent. Slowly and ever so quietly, I creep past a

56

stack of plastic boxes and a pile of old Fantastic Falcons banners and up the side of the tent. I can hear voices coming from inside and I crouch down to listen.

"I've made a big mistake," I can hear Andrew saying. "Anwen was never really mine to sell. She's Griff's bird. I know we had an arrangement, Rhys, but I think I should return your money and take Anwen back to Griff."

"All right then, Andrew," Rhys says. "Hand over the money."

"Well … the thing is …" I can hear Andrew stutter.

"You don't have it, do you?" barks Rhys. "No money, no bird."

I can hear Troy now. "But Dad, she doesn't even like it here."

"It doesn't matter whether she likes it here

or not," Rhys roars. "She's *my* bird. And once I've broken her in, she'll be the best of the bunch."

I just have enough time to jump behind the tent before Rhys and Andrew stride out of the front. "Let's look for him again."

I peer around the corner of the tent to see Rhys and Andrew walking off, having left Troy to guard the tent.

*This is my chance*, I tell myself. *It's now or never.* I creep back around the side of the tent and say, "Psst! Troy?"

He looks from side to side.

"Here," I say loudly.

Troy walks towards the sound of my voice.

"Listen to me, please, just for a minute? You're the only hope I've got, Troy, but if you don't like what I've got to say, I'll hand myself in. Deal?"

"All right," says Troy.

I step inside the tent. A musty odour

hits my nostrils. Despite the front flap being unzipped, the air inside is thick and humid. Daylight shines through its thinned nylon canvas. In one corner, there's a pop-up table with two big bird cages sitting on top of it. Another cage is lying on the grass beneath the table.

"Anwen!" I say, crouching down.

Troy clears his throat.

I turn around. "OK," I begin, feeling nervous. "You and your dad, you've been working with birds for a long time. You obviously know how to handle them?"

Troy nods slowly.

"So what makes Anwen so difficult?"

"I dunno," he shrugs. "Dad says some birds just are."

"Yeah. But what do *you* think?"

Troy stares down at his feet. Maybe no one's ever asked him what he thinks before.

"Look at my hands," I say, turning them over before him. "Anwen has never scratched me like she's scratched you and your dad. Why do you think that is?"

Troy's face falls. "Obvious, isn't it?" he mutters. "She's not happy. She's not meant for all this." He stares around the tent. "I've been trying to tell Dad that since we got her, but he won't listen. With the other birds, so long as they're being fed and flown and kept warm and safe, they don't mind the people, the noise, the photos. They've grown used to it. But I've told Dad a million times that Anwen's different. She's not like the other birds. She won't just grow into it because she hates it here. It's like there's somewhere else she needs to be – "

"Listen," I say. "We haven't got long, but I think you need to hear Anwen's story."

Troy leans back and nods.

"OK, so one night, my grandad's sitting at home minding his own business when he hears a sudden shrieking sound coming from the garden. He shoots outside and that's when he finds her – Anwen – she'd flown into a telephone wire and broken her wing."

Troy grimaces.

"So," I continue, "Grandad nurses her back to good health, even builds her a little bird-home in the woods behind our house. Anwen loves that little bird-home but, even more than that, she loves the shed at the bottom of our garden. Every evening, after dusk, she swoops by to visit Grandad there. To start with, he just throws her the odd strip of leftover meat but as the weeks pass, he starts giving her more and more, and as the years go by, they become best mates. Grandad transforms the shed for Anwen, builds her a proper home, and then he starts learning how to handle her. He flies her in the fields, and when I turn ten, he lets me in on it and starts teaching me too. But then – "

I stop, fighting the lump in my throat, knowing what comes next.

"And then what?" asks Troy.

"Well, then my grandad passes away," I say, feeling hot tears prickling behind my eyes.

"Oh," says Troy, looking awkward. "I'm sorry. He sounds like a great guy."

"Thanks," I say. "He was. These last couple of weeks have been the worst. But if it's this hard for me, can you imagine how difficult it must be for Anwen? I mean, she's grieving just like me."

"Oh, man," sighs Troy.

"Anwen is family," I say to him, "and that's why I've got to save her, Troy. That's why I've got to set her free."

Troy takes a step back and raises his hands in alarm. "Set her free?" he says. "That's a bad idea. Dad paid a lot of money for her, and I don't think Andrew can pay it back. Besides, if he found out I had anything to do with it, I'd be in so much trouble!"

"I've got an idea," I say. "But for it to work, I'm going to need your help."

# Chapter 7

I pull the zip of Troy's tweed jacket up to my chin, while he pulls my coat – now turned the proper way around – over his shoulders.

"Perfect," I say, giving him a thumbs-up.

While I open Anwen's cage, Troy peeks his head out of the tent, watching for Andrew and Rhys.

"No sign of them," he says.

I gently remove Anwen's hood. She blinks a couple of times, cocks her head from left to right and then stares at me with a piercing yellow eye.

"Hello, Anwen," I say, holding out a treat for her. "I'm here."

While she tears and picks at the meat, I gently rub my fingernail over her talon – something Grandad used to do to make her relax.

Once she's finished, she hops from the perch onto my glove without me even asking.

"Someone wants to get out of here fast, don't they?" I say, slowly carrying her from the cage to my chest where she starts to nestle her head.

"They're heading this way," Troy says.

"You remember the plan, right?"

"I'm going to run out of the tent, towards the café and I'm going to keep on running."

"Let's just hope they take the bait," I say, biting my bottom lip.

"They will," replies Troy, nodding.

"And what are you going to say if they catch you?"

"If they catch me, I'm going to tell them that you snuck up on me and took my coat and Anwen. Then I'll tell them that I put your coat on because it might rain again, and ran out to try and catch you."

"OK," I say, suddenly feeling breathless. "Then I'll release Anwen and try and explain to Mum again."

Troy nods. "Goodbye, Anwen," he says. "Good luck, Griff."

We peek through the entrance. Rhys and Andrew are talking to the woman at the medieval combat training tent. I can see Mum sitting down at the café with her head in her hands. A pang of guilt shoots through me but I haven't got time to think about her right now.

"Ready?" I say to Troy.

"Ready," he says, taking a few deep breaths.

"Three, two, one – go!"

Troy rockets out of the tent and shoots across the lawn. I watch as Andrew and Rhys spot him and immediately give chase.

I collect Anwen's hood from the table, pull it over her head, and tuck her inside Troy's coat, to conceal her and to protect her from the wind.

"OK, Anwen," I say. "Here we go!"

I sneak around the corner of the tent, back the way I came, and down the slope to the dense bushes. Then I bend to my knees and unhood her.

"Right, Anwen," I say. "This is it."

I unclip her jesses – the short leather straps fastened around each of her legs – and hold my arm out.

"Come on, girl."

I watch her, careful not to blink and miss what could be our final moment together. But she just stares at me.

"Come on, now," I whisper. "Go. This is your chance."

But rather than taking flight, she hops to the crook of my arm and buries her head into my chest again.

"I know, I know," I say, feeling a mix of panic and frustration. "But please, Anwen, you've got to go. You've got to fly away."

*It's only a matter of time till they find me,* I tell myself.

"Come on, now, Anwen. You *need* to fly away."

But nothing. She just stands there, glued to my glove.

And now the panic really does start to set in. *What if she doesn't go? What if she doesn't fly away? She isn't going to do it, is she? After all this, she isn't going to fly away! She's too afraid. She doesn't want to be alone.*

Just then, a thick drizzle begins to fall. *It's over,* I tell myself. *It's over. I'm all alone and I'm aching and I'm cold and I'm wet. And I've let Anwen down. I've let Grandad down.*

*Grandad ... What would he say if he could see me now?*

I stare up at the sky feeling more helpless and miserable than I've ever felt in all my life.

*Wait a minute ... Grandad knew Anwen better than anybody. He knew falconry. He'd know exactly what to do ... How would he get her to fly?* I try to remember every little scrap of information Grandad ever told me about falcons.

"*Did you know, Griff, that falcons are the fastest animals in the world? That's right, they can dive at speeds of up to 320 kilometres per hour!*"

"*Did you know that falcons are named after their own claws? That's true, that is. You see, 'falcon' comes from the Latin name 'falco', which means sickle. You know what a sickle is, right? No! You don't? Right – to the shed!*"

"*If you're ever having trouble flying a falcon, Griff, you must reach for higher ground because the higher a falcon is, the more comfortable they are.*"

*That's what I need!* I realise. *I need to get higher up!*

*Thank you, Grandad! Thank you!*

Just then, I hear a loud noise coming from outside the big brown tent. When I look up over the bushes, my breath catches in my throat. Rhys is marching Troy towards the tent.

"I told you what happened," I can hear Troy wailing. "He overpowered me."

Rhys disappears inside the tent, leaving Andrew and Troy outside.

A moment later, Rhys bursts out of the tent, shouting, "He's stolen her. Your boy's stolen my bird!" He starts taking deep, angry breaths. "You need to make this right, Andrew. Right now."

"I will," says Andrew. "Just calm down."

"Calm down?" snaps Rhys. "Ha! Not likely!"

Rhys spots me and then starts running in my direction.

Unable to stop myself, I utter a frightened cry. Then something surprising happens.

# Chapter 8

Andrew dives between Rhys and me, and Rhys pushes Andrew to the ground.

I burst out of the bushes, run along the gravel path and jump up onto the grassy lawn. Then, I sprint towards the highest point in Denbigh Castle, the White Chamber Tower.

*I only hope it will be high enough for Anwen to fly away!*

I slip and slide on the wet grass, all the while keeping Anwen tucked tight into my chest.

I glance briefly over my shoulder to see Rhys running towards me. He's holding a toy wooden axe.

As if sensing my panic, Anwen gives a quick squawk.

"Nothing to fear," I tell her.

Just then, Mum spots me. She starts waving her arms, but I can't stop now.

I charge through the entrance and then up some steep stone steps. There are two thick walls on either side. The wall on the right has half-tumbled away. Rain comes crashing down through the gap and onto my head. There's no time even to flinch as icy cold water runs down my back. I take the steep steps two at a time, trying my best to side-step pools of water collecting at my feet, knowing that one slip could end everything. On my right is a handrail, which I use to hoist myself up until I come to a heavy metal gate. But it's closed.

I look for another way through, but I can hear the slapping of Rhys's feet coming up the stairs. I've no choice but to run towards the gate.

*It's locked! But it's just a slide lock. I should be able to open it. But is there time?*

I try to slide the bolt to the left, but it's stuck. I pull and pull and pull and any second now Rhys is going to grab me when –

At last, it shifts. I pull the heavy gate open, squeeze through and close it behind me.

BANG!

Rhys's hand slams onto the heavy gate, knocking me over. He makes a sudden lunge, grasping through the bars. His fingers brush against my chest but they fall short of actually seizing the front of Troy's coat. Poor Anwen gives another loud squawk.

Then, Rhys starts yanking at the gate. Instinctively, I press my foot against one of the bars and push as hard as I can. The momentum of his pull and my push sends the gate flying open, which in turn sends him flying backwards, slipping on the stone and then crashing to the floor.

I set off again, up more stone steps onto another platform. On either side of me, light seeps through giant cannon-like holes in the walls. To the left, is the car park, St Hilary's Chapel and a view of the town. To the right, I can see the grassy lawn. Rain is pelting down onto a small crowd of children and adults who are all staring up at me, confused.

I splash my way along the platform and almost lose my footing as four descending steps seem to appear out of nowhere.

*With a bit of luck,* I think, *Rhys might just lose his footing here and knock himself out cold!*

To the right, my path continues upwards. Twenty metres away, I can see my destination: the very top of the White Chamber Tower. In the middle of the tower, stands the flagpole with the Welsh flag on it, still blowing in the wind.

As I make my way towards it, the path gets even steeper, and even more slippery. Steel railings give way to a wooden stairwell, which goes even higher, and I can feel the wind now pushing me this way and that, as I run along the highest platform. To my right, nine metres below, a growing crowd of people are staring up, wide-eyed and open-mouthed, some pointing upwards. A sudden gust of wind lifts me off my feet and someone in the crowd below lets out a shrill cry. I clutch the wooden banister and wait for the wind to pass.

When the wind subsides, I dash straight past the flagpole and climb over the safety fence. I know it's a dangerous thing to do with the wet and the wind, but I figure it might just buy me the time I need to release Anwen.

I unzip Troy's coat, take Anwen out and unhood her.

"Right, Anwen," I say. "This is it, girl. Last chance."

I hold her out on my arm. She's free to take off at any time.

Just then, Rhys stumbles across the wooden platform and sets his giant hands on either side of the safety barrier. His angry green eyes burn into mine once more as he hobbles forwards.

"That's *my* bird!" he shouts. My knees almost buckle under the force of his angry bellow. "You get her tethered and hand her over right now – or else!"

Gathering my courage, I hold his stare and say: "Or else what?"

He steps over the safety barrier.

"Stay back," I warn. I step back, the heel of my trainer hanging over the edge of the ridge. My foot dislodges some loose stones and bits of grit that tumble to the ground below. And, all of a sudden, my heart is thumping in my chest, harder than ever before.

Just then, out of the corner of my eye, I see a small group of people dashing towards us, including Mum, Troy, Andrew and two police officers.

Rhys doesn't see any of this. His angry expression drops into a horrible sneer. "You give me my falcon," he hisses.

"She's not yours," I tell him. "She's not mine or anybody else's."

"Get away from my son!" cries Mum, running towards the safety barrier.

"Sir!" calls one of the police officers. "I need you to climb back over the safety rail!"

"Right now!" says the other officer.

Rhys ignores them and takes another step towards me.

I take another step back and extend my arm out to its fullest.

"Griff, what are you doing?" shouts Mum.

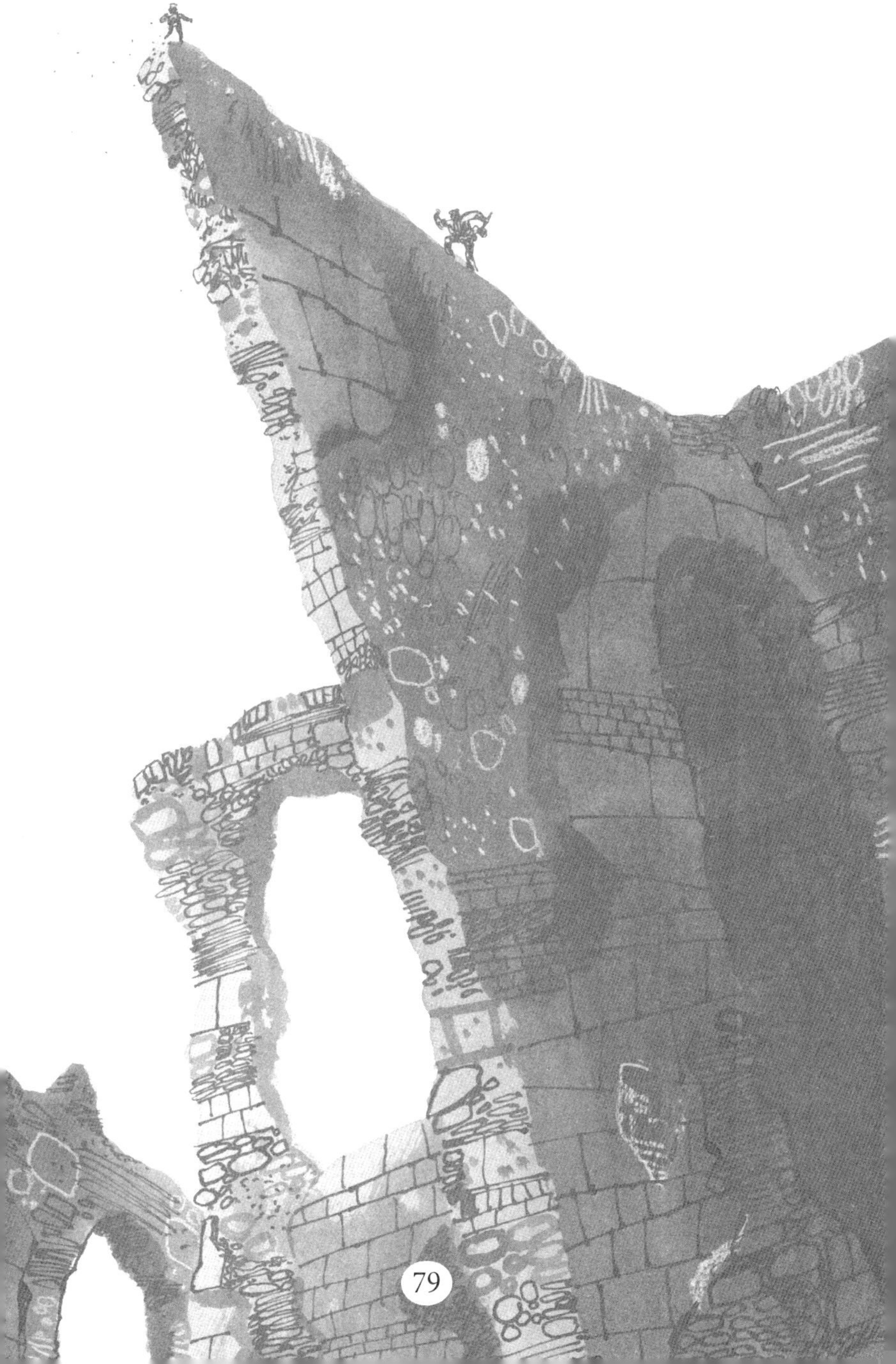

"I'm letting Anwen choose," I say, struggling to keep my balance. "If she flies to Rhys or to Troy, then so be it, but if she flies back to me or if she flies away, then that's her choice."

"No!" calls Rhys, reaching forwards. "NO!"

I kiss Anwen on the back of her head, whisper "good girl" into her ear and then cast my arm out, forcing her to take flight.

She swoops into a six-metre dive and pulls up just over the heads of the crowd. In two blinks, she's veering away, a speck in the distance; then she wheels back around and begins to return.

"See?" roars Rhys, with a laugh. "She's coming back! She's coming back!"

But Anwen soars straight past us and, just like that, she disappears behind a wall. Gone. Free.

Rhys's face hardens. Then I notice the corner of his mouth is twitching.

*What's he planning?* I wonder.

"Sir, I won't ask you again," calls the first police officer. "I need you to climb back over the safety rail, right now!"

"Of course, officer," replies Rhys, holding his hands up in the air. "I was only trying to help this poor boy here. I mean, you all saw what happened. He stole my bird – a bird I paid good money for, mind – and then he let her go. I mean, if that's not theft, I don't know what is!"

"That's all very interesting, sir," says the police officer, signalling her fellow officer to help me back over the safety barrier. "But I'm not here about Anwen," she continues.

At the sound of Anwen's name, Rhys's knees visibly shake.

"Oh, yes," she continues. "I knew Griff's grandad very well. He worked on the police force before he retired and took up falconry. But that's beside the point. I'm here right now because of a report of an altercation between yourself and Andrew Connors this afternoon. And it appears you're carrying an axe, which 14 witnesses say you've been waving menacingly."

Rhys starts to briefly protest, but then the other police officer says, "We also have reports of out-of-control birds of prey, and a refusal to return money to a customer."

Rhys's shoulders slump and the police lead him away for questioning.

"Griff!" says Mum, pulling me into a big bear hug. "Don't you – ever do – anything – like that – ever – again," she snaps. "You had me worried sick!"

"I'm sorry, Mum," I say. "I didn't have a choice."

"I know, I know," she says.

We make it down the steep stairs and back to the main lawn. Troy's standing near the police van, looking miserable. "Are you OK?" I ask.

"I will be," he says, nodding. "My aunt's on her way to pick me up now. Someone from the RSPB is here, too. They're going to look after the birds."

"Thanks again for all your help," I say. "There's no way I could have done it without you."

"I know," says Troy, holding out his hand. "I'll have my coat back, if that's OK. And the glove."

I give him back his coat and the glove, and he hands over my coat. *Castles of North Wales* is still in the pocket.

"I hope Anwen's happier now," Troy says. "See you around, Griff."

"See you," I say.

And just like that, Rhys, Troy and the police officers leave. Andrew, Mum and I stand there and watch them go.

Just when I think the excitement has come to an end, Mum turns to Andrew and says, "Right, now that's over, I think you and I need a word – "

## Chapter 9

The crowd of people who were standing on the lawn watching the drama unfold start moving away, and getting back to their own business. But there's still tension in the air as Mum leads the way along the gravel path, skirting the lawn, until we reach a quiet spot.

Mum and I watch as Andrew drags his heels towards us. He's wearing his usual hangdog expression, and he doesn't wait to hear what Mum has to say. Instead – in typical Andrew-style – he starts trying to dig himself out of this fresh new hole he's dug. "Please, Delyth," he begins. "I know I've made a big, big mistake – "

Mum holds up her hand, which makes Andrew

stop talking. "A big mistake," she says. "Just the one, Andrew? See, I don't think I have enough fingers on my hands to count the number of mistakes that you've made today. Or lies you've told."

Andrew starts to protest, but Mum silences him with a look.

"You've lied about Anwen," she continues. "You've lied about having a new job. You lied about Griff's reaction to seeing Anwen. You lied to Griff! Everything bad that's happened today is your fault."

"I'm sorry," he says.

"Thank you," replies Mum. "But I'm not the only one you need to apologise to."

"I'm sorry, Griff," says Andrew. "I was just trying to fix things."

He does genuinely seem to mean it, but I think it's too little, too late. "The problem is," I say, "you weren't trying to fix things for me, or Mum. You were just thinking about yourself."

"That's not fair," he protests.

"Let him speak," snaps Mum.

"It's not just what's happened today. It's not just all your actions and lies. It's the way you talk to people – Mum and me. Home just isn't home anymore, not with you in it. You don't take responsibility for anything. Everyone walks on eggshells when you're around, because no one knows when you're next going to lose your temper. When Grandad was with us, at least he kept you in check."

"But Grandad's not here anymore," adds Mum.

"No," murmurs Andrew.

For a moment, nobody says anything.

Then Mum says, "You can drive us all back to the house, and then it's time we went our separate ways."

I look up at Mum, feeling pleasantly shocked.

Andrew doesn't say anything. He stares at us both for a moment and then nods. Eventually, he says, "You're right, Delyth. Griff, your mum's right. I'm just really, really sorry – "

# Chapter 10

That evening, Mum and I are making our way down to the shed at the bottom of our garden. Sorting the shed was one of the last things Grandad did before he died. All around it, there's a small square of ground covered with whitewashed slabs, on top of which sit two neat rows of raised beds, containing carrots, dwarf beans and courgettes. The roof and side of the shed have been patched neatly with lengths of tarpaulin, and the door has been freshly painted.

I'm carrying Grandad's little paraffin stove. I found it in the garage in a cardboard box, which Andrew had labelled "Junk".

Mum's carrying two steaming cups of hot

chocolate. "Now, don't get your hopes up too high about Anwen returning," she tells me.

"I doubt she'll come back, Mum," I say, opening the door and stepping inside. "To be honest, I'm just happy she got away. I think that's what Grandad would have wanted."

"Yeah," says Mum, pulling me in for a hug. "Me too."

A few moments later, we're both sitting down, listening to the wind blowing outside. I'm sitting on Grandad's rocking chair, which we brought down from the house earlier, while Mum's taken the comfy armchair. It's so nice and cosy and peaceful. As I rock gently, back and forth, I can really understand why Grandad spent so much time inside here. And yet, every minute or so, I find my eyes flitting over to the empty T-shaped perch on the shelf at the far end of the shed.

*She won't come back*, I tell myself. *There's no way. It's impossible. How would she even find her way back? She's probably flying around right now searching for her dinner, having the time of her life …*

Mum must have noticed I've gone quiet because she says, "Maybe, in time, we could look at getting you a falcon of your own? You've got all the equipment and all the know-how. I think you'd be a wonderful falconer."

"Maybe," I say, slurping my hot chocolate, thinking of Grandad. "Yeah, I think I'd like that."

And for a moment, we just sit there, lost in our thoughts.

I stare out over the fields. It's dark now, but at the far end, I can just about make out the wooden post that Grandad used to train Anwen. I remember the story he told me of Anwen's first flight without a creance. He'd been training her with the creance for two weeks straight, and it was finally time for him to try her without it, but he couldn't.

He was scared she'd fly away.

For a whole week, he kept putting it off because he felt sick with nerves. But then, one afternoon, he just went for it. He marched out into the field. He placed Anwen on that wooden post, and he turned his back and walked away, not knowing whether she'd still be there when he got to the middle of the field to call her.

He said it was the longest walk of his entire life. But once there, he simply turned around, called her and Anwen shot towards him, landing on his glove and nestling into his chest before he could let out a single breath. Grandad said that moment was up there with the most thrilling and terrifying experiences he'd ever had in his entire life. I guess that's what made me so interested in falconry, so eager and so inspired – Grandad.

"Griff," says Mum. She's smiling but I can hear sadness in her voice. "I want you to know, I'm sorry."

"Mum," I say. "What do you have to be sorry for?"

"Everything," she says, putting her mug on the floor. "Andrew, mainly. I'm really sorry he made you feel that way. I'm sorry I didn't listen to you. Not just today. Right from the start."

"That's OK," I reply, putting my hand on hers. "I should have been a better talker."

"No, Griff," she says, sternly. "This is on me, not you. From now on, we need to talk to one another and share things. You and I are a team, Griff. You're the most important person in my life."

"And you're mine, too," I tell her. "Hey! Guess what?" I say, changing the subject. "I've learnt some things today."

"And what have you learnt, love?" she asks.

I try to think of how best to say it. "Hmm, it's hard to explain, but I guess, just because somebody acts in a bad way, it doesn't necessarily mean that they're a bad person. Like Andrew standing between Rhys and me, when Rhys was angry. I really didn't expect him to do that. So, people can do good things and bad things."

"That's very wise, Griff," says Mum, smiling.

I finish my hot chocolate and put the mug on the floor. "And then the second thing," I say, "is something Grandad told me. He said sometimes humans think that they're better than animals, but we're not, and he said that we should always treat animals with love and respect. I guess that's what I wanted for Anwen, really. Love and respect."

At these words, a big grey blur whooshes into the shed through the open window, making Mum and me jump. It lands on the T-perch. And then, just like that, it *snaps* into focus before me.

I blink once, twice. I can't believe my eyes. I turn to Mum in utter astonishment to find her looking back at me in much the same way.

Standing proudly before us with her wings outstretched, exposing her pale cross-barred-with-dark-brown breast, is Anwen.

I almost fall out of the rocking chair.

"Anwen?" I cry. "It's you!"

I jump to my feet, walk over and stroke her breast feathers.

Anwen hops to the crook of my arm, just like she used to do with Grandad, just like she did earlier, and she buries her head into my chest.

Mum walks over, places her arm on my shoulder, and time seems to float away as we stand together for seconds, minutes, hours, I don't know.

Then, strange as it may seem, Mum and I both say the exact same words at the exact same time, and it's clear that we're talking to each other, as well as Anwen when we say,

"Welcome home."

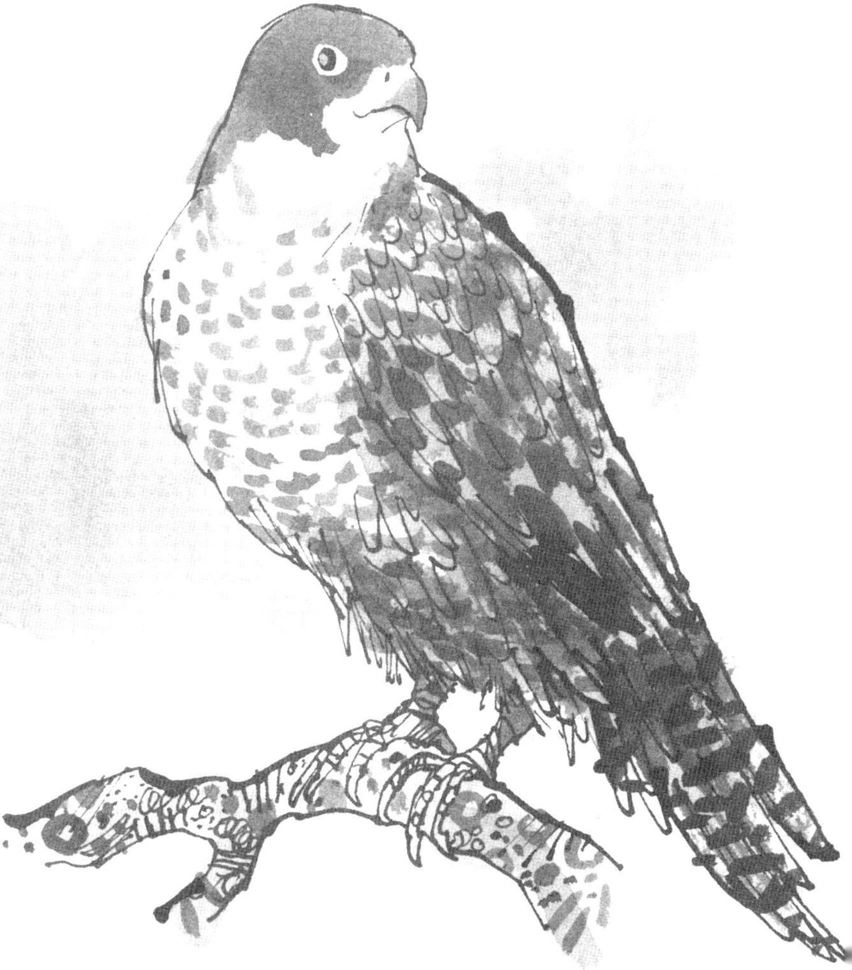

# Book talk questions

Do you think Troy wants to help out at Fantastic Falcons?

How does Griff's connection to his grandfather influence him throughout the book?

Why do you think Andrew acts the way he does?

How did you feel while reading the story?

Have you ever felt very connected to an animal?

Do you think it's right that birds and other animals are attractions at events?

Why do you think Griff is so attached to Anwen?

How do you think Mum feels at the end of the book?

Did your opinion of any characters change by the time you finished the book?

Do you think that Anwen will come back to Griff's house again?

# Ask the author

**How did you first get into writing?**

As a child, I read a lot with my dad. This inspired me to write poems and stories of my own, as well as performing plays for my friends and family. I then studied Theatre at university.

In 2015, I co-founded a writing and outreach organisation called Stories Of Care. It was here that I discovered my passion and flair for writing stories for children and young people.

*Oliver Sykes*

**What was your inspiration for writing this story?**

My partner Gwen inspired this story. She took me to visit Denbigh Castle during the Medieval Festival. As we were walking along, I recalled that my dad had taken my siblings and me to a Horse Fair where I was allowed to fly a peregrine falcon. It was this awe-inspiring experience, and the vividness of the memory, that sowed the seeds of *Saving Anwen*.

**What's your favourite thing about being an author?**
I love everything, really. I love the preparatory work that goes into planning a story. I love sitting down and actually writing stories and I love collaborating with editorial and design teams to make my stories the best they can be and turn them into actual books.

**What book did you most enjoy as a child?**
*Danny the Champion of the World* by Roald Dahl was a book that changed my life by turning me into an avid reader but *A Kestrel for a Knave* by Barry Hines is one I also really related to and enjoyed. It's a bittersweet story about a troubled teen in a Yorkshire mining town whose life is transformed through raising a hawk – Kes.

**What do you think comes next for Griff and Anwen?**
On the one hand, I think Griff and Anwen could live happily ever after. But on the other, I think it would be interesting if Anwen failed to come home and Griff had to search for her, past the woods, deep into the wilderness.

**Collins**
**BIG CAT**

Published by Collins
An imprint of HarperCollins*Publishers*

The News Building
1 London Bridge Street
London SE1 9GF
UK

Macken House
39/40 Mayor Street Upper
Dublin 1
D01 C9W8
Ireland

© HarperCollins*Publishers* Limited 2025

10 9 8 7 6 5 4 3 2 1

ISBN 978-0-00-874483-0

All rights reserved. No part of this publication may be reproduced, stored in a retrieval system, or transmitted in any form by any means, electronic, mechanical, photocopying, recording or otherwise, without the prior written permission of the Publisher or a licence permitting restricted copying in the United Kingdom issued by the Copyright Licensing Agency Ltd, 5th Floor, Shackleton House, 4 Battle Bridge Lane, London SE1 2HX.

Without limiting the author's and publisher's exclusive rights, any unauthorised use of this publication to train generative artificial intelligence (AI) technologies is expressly prohibited. HarperCollins also exercise their rights under Article 4(3) of the Digital Single Market Directive 2019/790 and expressly reserve this publication from the text and data mining exception.

British Library Cataloguing-in-Publication Data
A catalogue record for this publication is available from the British Library.

Author: Oliver Sykes
Illustrator: Ian Morris (Spring Literary)
Publisher: Laura White
Commissioning editor: Holly Woolnough
Development editor: Zoë Clarke
Product manager: Holly Woolnough
Content editor: Selin Akca
Copyeditor: Sally Byford
Proofreader: Catherine Dakin
Reviewer: Lisa Davis
Cover designer: Sarah Finan
Internal design: 2Hoots Publishing Services Ltd
Typesetter: Jouve India Ltd
Production controller: Katharine Willard

p100 © Dawn Kilner Photography

Collins would like to thank the teachers and children at Grange Primary School, Southwark, for being part of the development of Big Cat Read On.

Printed in the UK

**MIX**
Paper | Supporting responsible forestry
FSC™ C007454

This book contains FSC™ certified paper and other controlled sources to ensure responsible forest management.

For more information visit: www.harpercollins.co.uk/green

Made with responsibly sourced paper and vegetable ink

Scan to see how we are reducing our environmental impact.

**Get the latest Collins Big Cat news at**
collins.co.uk/collinsbigcat

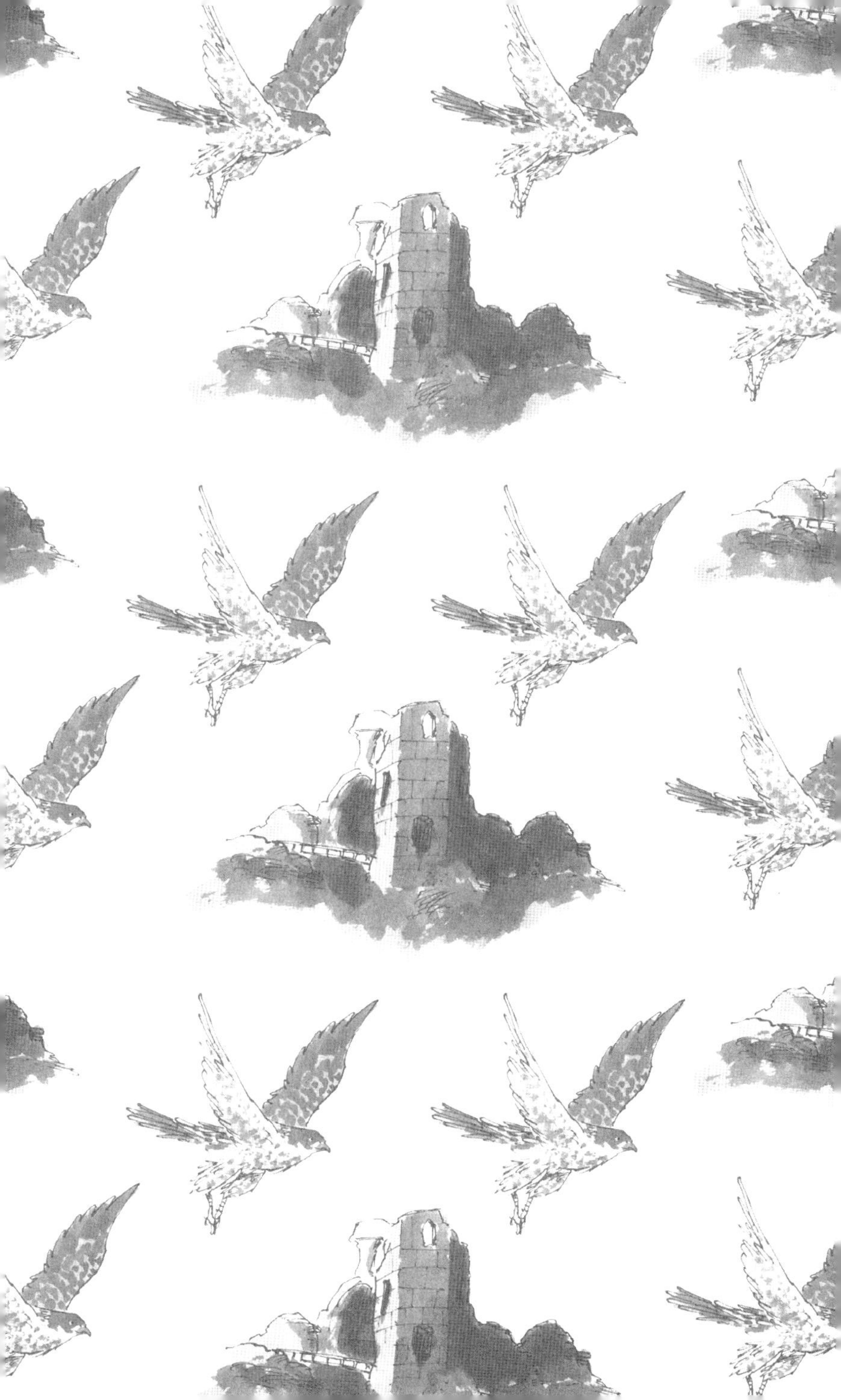

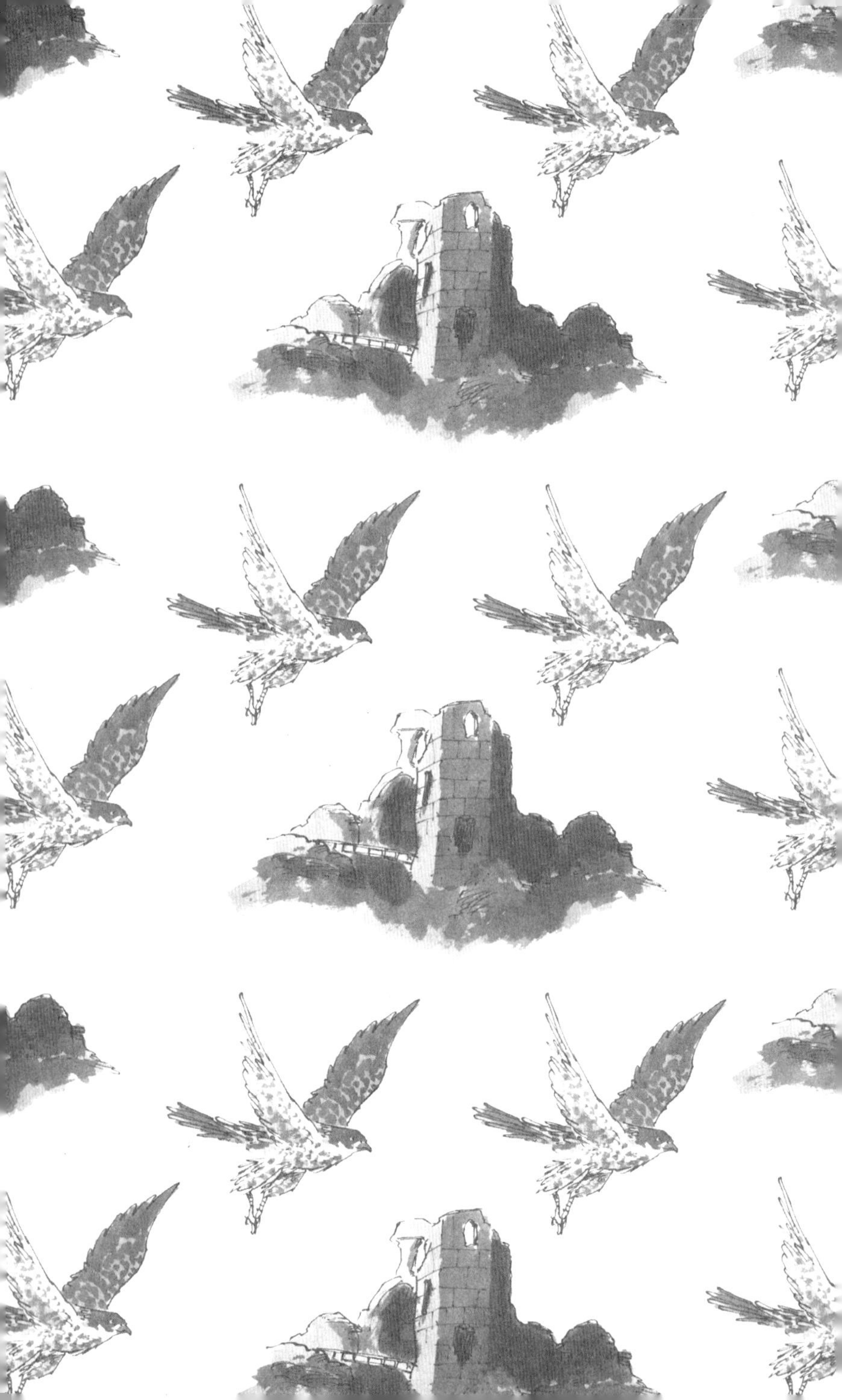